Babar's Day Out

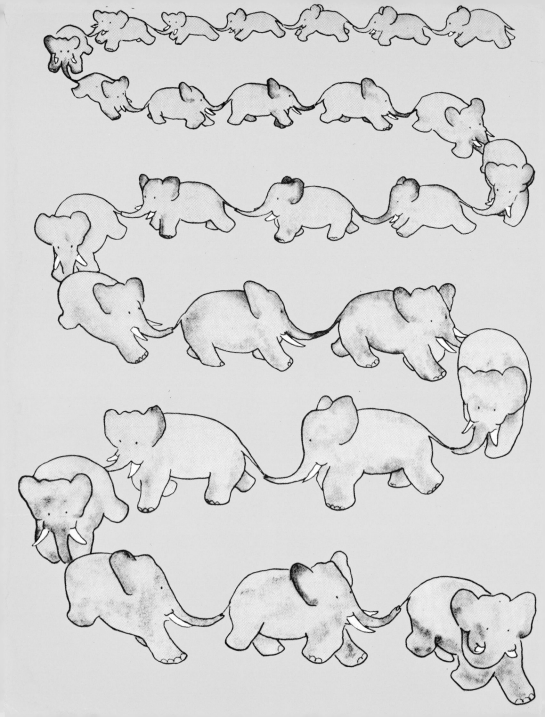

LAURENT DE BRUNHOFF

BABAR'S
DAY OUT

A MAGNET BOOK

One day Babar set off in the car for a picnic
with Celeste and the children. Arthur
and Zephir perched on the trailer, next
to the food and the barbecue.
"Don't eat our lunch on the way!"
Pom called to them.
"Oh yes, we shall," joked Arthur. "I
love tomatoes."

"And I like hard-boiled eggs," added Zephir. Pom was furious, and Celeste tried to calm him down. "Don't worry, they're only teasing you," she told him.

As they drove past a wood Celeste said,
"Don't let's go any further. This will do."
Babar stopped, and they arranged their
picnic. Celeste sliced the tomatoes and said,
"Pom, bring me the plates, please."
Arthur was proud of the way he had prepared the
skewers of meat.

Babar had lit a charcoal fire. Flora and
Alexander carried the skewers to him, and
he cooked them on the barbecue. Babar was
a very good cook.
"We must hurry," he said. "The first ones
are done already."
"Here are some more," said the children.
"All right. Put the cooked ones on a
plate. The fire is going well; it won't
take a minute to finish the rest."

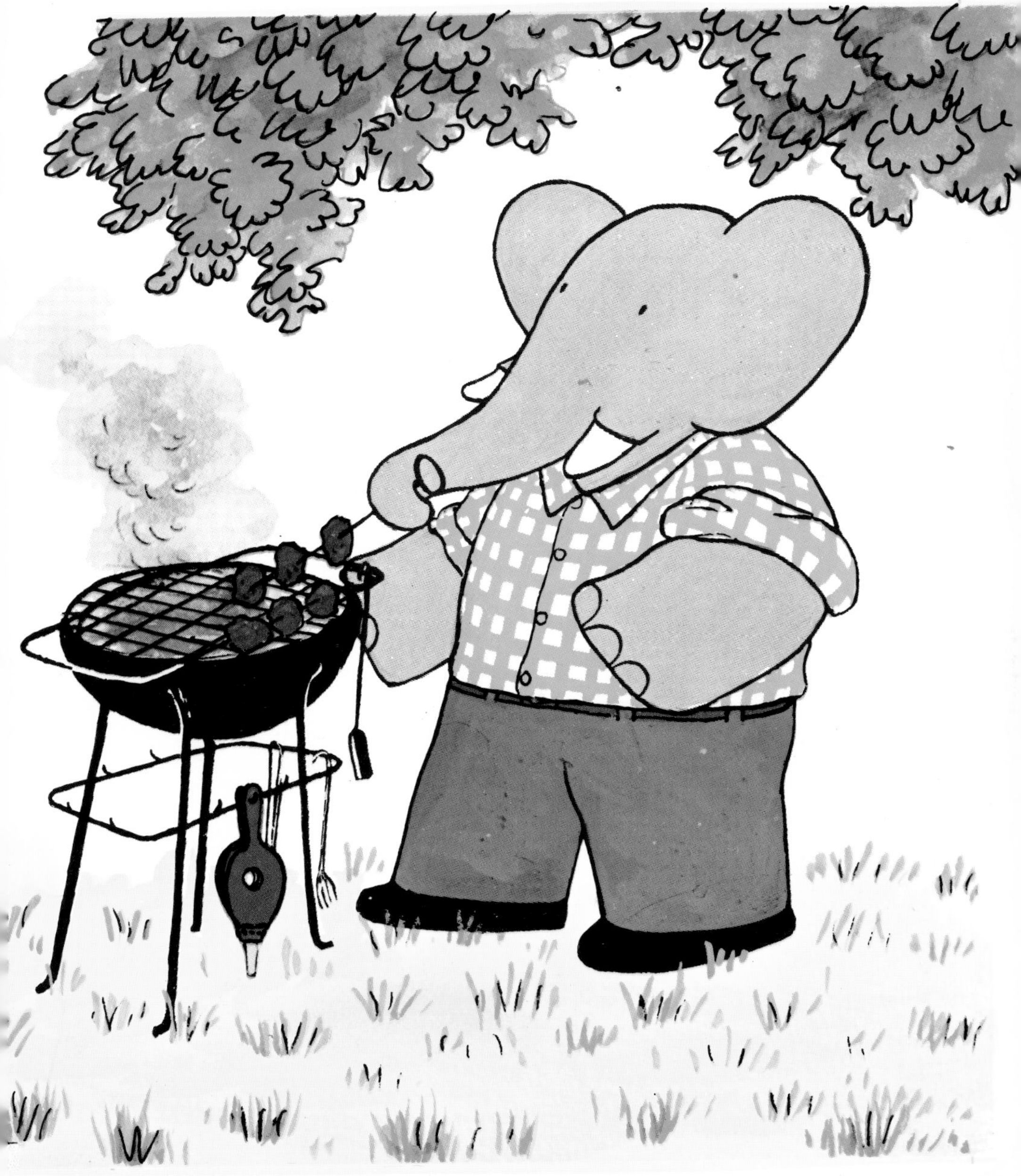

Arthur was hungry and ate a second helping.
His friend Zephir devoured a whole plate
of hard-boiled eggs. Arthur made fun
of him because he had stuffed his mouth
too full. "Say 'Papa'," he said teasingly.
But Zephir couldn't even open his mouth. . . .

"Goodness, just look at those ants!"
Pom tried to chase them off with
a table-napkin. "Oh, you nasty greedy
things!" he cried.
"Mind! They're on the bread!"
"If only we'd got some tomato leaves,"
said Zephir. "Ants hate them. They
go away if you put them on their route."
"What funny things you know," said Arthur.

For pudding Celeste had made a cherry
tart, but the wasps were attracted by the
sugar. Bzzz . . . Bzzz . . Bzzz!
"It's quite impossible to have lunch
in peace here. The wasps are just as
greedy as the ants."
"Look out, Flora," cried Pom.
Flora was just going to eat a slice
of tart. She was very frightened of
wasps, and flapped her ears to and fro.
"Go away! Go away! Oh!" Poor Flora
had been stung on the ear
by a wasp.

Alexander wandered off and got into the
car. He pretended he was a racing driver.
"I'm in second place!" he cried excitedly.
"But I'm going faster and faster! Brrroum!
I'm passing everyone else. I'm the winner!"
Suddenly the brake was released and the
car rolled gently down the slope. Pom
saw what was happening.
"Papa!" he cried, terrified.

The car was gaining speed.
Alexander didn't know how to stop it.
Pom, rooted to the spot with
horror, saw the car
plunge into a hollow and
his brother somersault
into a bush. . . .

Alexander fell among the leaves—
and the birds flew out!

Fortunately Alexander wasn't hurt. But
the car was stuck fast. Babar and
Arthur tried to pull it out with a rope.

"Heave . . . Heave . . .!"
Nothing happened.
The car wouldn't move
an inch.

"There's only one thing we can do," said
Babar. "We must walk back to a garage."
They all stepped out bravely behind
Babar. Alexander was patched up with
sticking-plaster. Flora's ear was still
burning hot with the wasp sting.
To make matters worse, the sun was already
sinking behind the trees.
"Left, right, left, right," said Arthur.
"Let's sing to help us along. . . ."

"Oh, the grand old Duke of York,
He had ten thousand men. . . ."

"There's the garage," said Babar.
"Now we'll soon be home!"

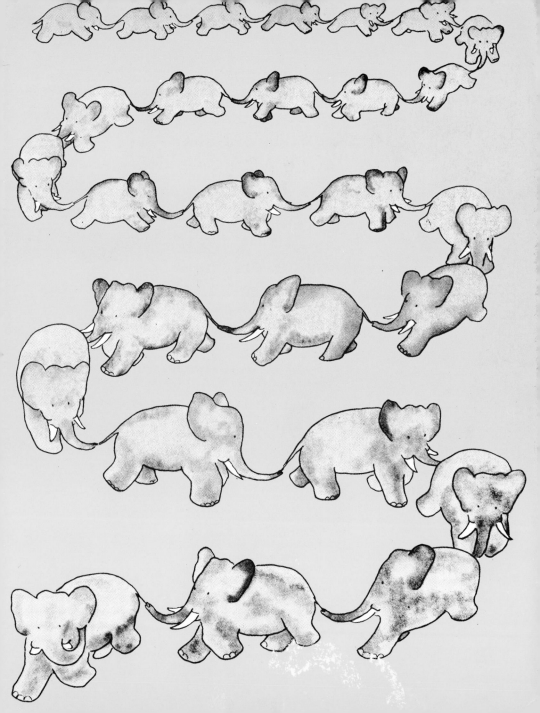

Little Babar Picture Paperbacks
in Magnet Books

Jean de Brunhoff

**The Story of Babar
Babar and the Crocodile**

Laurent de Brunhoff

**Babar the Gardener
Babar the Sportsman
Babar in the Snow
Babar at the Seaside
Babar Goes Camping
Babar's Day Out
Babar the Pilot
Babar the Musician
Babar and the Doctor
Babar the Cook
Babar and the Christmas Tree**

First published in Great Britain 1971 by Methuen & Co Ltd
First published by Librairie Hachette as *Babar en promenade*
Magnet edition first published 1980
by Methuen Children's Books Ltd
11 New Fetter Lane, London EC4P 4EE
Reprinted 1985
Copyright © 1966 Librairie Hachette
English translation copyright © 1971 Methuen & Co Ltd
Printed in Great Britain by
Hazell Watson & Viney Limited,
Member of the BPCC Group,
Aylesbury, Bucks
ISBN 0 416 88680 9